Seeds

Carme Lemniscates

CANDLEWICK STUDIO
an imprint of Candlewick Press

Seeds carry the power of life.
So they embark on amazing adventures.

Some take off to distant lands.

Others wait to be carried to their destiny.

Once they find their place, seeds go through breathtaking transformations.

Seeds have the power to multiply in number:
one pumpkin seed brings dozens of pumpkins.

And each pumpkin brings hundreds of seeds!

Seeds have the power to multiply in size. The tiniest seed in the world sprouts a beautiful orchid.

Seeds have the power to grow in difficult places.
They can thrive despite all odds.

When we sow a seed, we take part in this amazing cycle.

And we can plant many different kinds of seeds.
A smile is a powerful seed.

One that can bring joy and friendship.

But there are also seeds that bring anger and misunderstanding.
When those seeds grow, they pull us apart.

Seeds can only bring what they carry.
Pumpkin seeds bring pumpkins; kindness seeds bring kindness.

You have lots of seeds, and you get to decide which ones to plant and which ones to help grow.

Seeds have whole worlds inside them,
just like you.

First edition 2020. Library of Congress Catalog Card Number 2020901917. ISBN 978-1-5362-0844-3. This book was typeset in Lunchbox. The illustrations were done in mixed media.
Candlewick Studio, an imprint of Candlewick Press, 99 Dover Street, Somerville, Massachusetts 02144. www.candlewickstudio.com.
Printed in Heshan, Guangdong, China. 23 24 LEO 10 9 8 7 6 5 4 3